MARY HAD A LITTLE LAB

Sue Fliess   pictures by Petros Bouloubasis

Albert Whitman & Company
Chicago, Illinois

For female inventors everywhere—SF

To Sophia and Jason—PB

Library of Congress Cataloging-in-Publication data is on file with the publisher.

Text copyright © 2018 by Sue Fliess
Pictures copyright © 2018 by Albert Whitman & Company
Pictures by Petros Bouloubasis
Published in 2018 by Albert Whitman & Company
ISBN 978-0-8075-4982-7
Printed in China
10 9 8 7 6 5 4 3 2 1 HH 22 21 20 19 18 17

Design by Ellen Kokontis

For more information about Albert Whitman & Company,
visit our website at www.albertwhitman.com.

Mary had a little lab.
She tested and created.
While other kids were at the park,
she built and calculated.

Inventing can be lonely, though.
She rarely stopped for fun.
One day she thought she'd call a friend...
but couldn't think of one.

"Maybe I just need a pet!
One fluffy, soft, and sweet.
To snuggle, cuddle, hold, and love,
and make my life complete."

She traveled to a local farm
with scissors and a sack.

She snipped a tiny tuft of wool,

then quickly headed back.

She made an apparatus
with pulleys, knobs, and gears.
Then set the switches, pipes, and springs,
and covered both her ears.

SHEEPINATOR

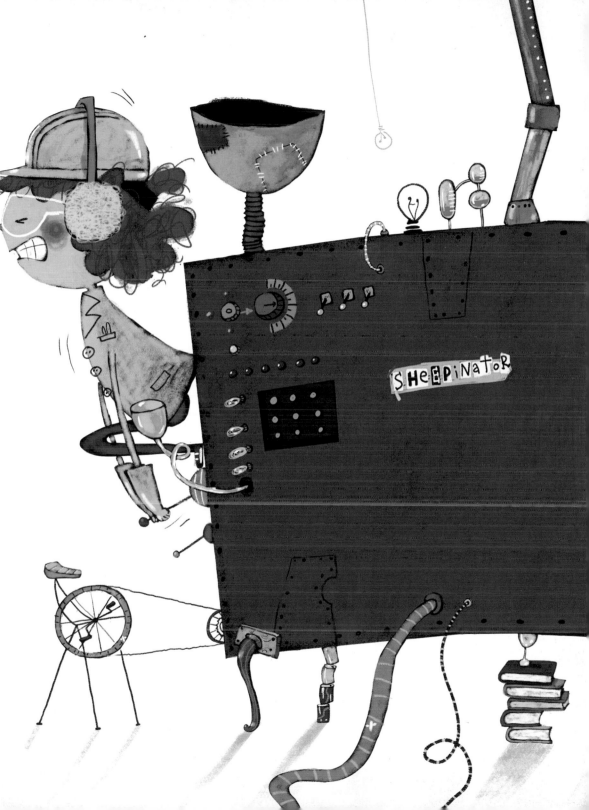

"The new machine is finished!
My best invention ever!"
Then Mary turned the power on
and gently pulled the lever.

She pushed the wool
into the chute

and poured the mixture in...

Then pumped the pedals with her feet
to give it all a spin.

"I have a pet to keep!"
The brilliant budding scientist
had made a woolly sheep!

The sheep assisted in the lab
and often helped with chores.

He carried all the groceries

and buffed the kitchen floors.

He followed her to school one day.
The teacher was impressed.
He said the sheep could stay in class
as Mary's special guest.

The kids all rushed to see the sheep
and asked if they could play.
"Oh, Mary, could we have one too?"

"I'll make you some today!"

She led them to her little lab.
"Behold! The Sheepinator!"

SHEEPINATOR

"I simply press this button here:
the woolly duplicator."

But soon the duplicator jammed;
the sheep dropped out in twos.

They filled the lab,
    the yard,
        the street...
They made the evening news!

The town was overrun with sheep!
She'd made ten times a flock.
The wool went on for miles and miles,
'round every city block.

Mary said, "Let's fix this jam!"
They pulled until it popped.

SHEEPINATOR

Then flipped the whole thing upside down…
until, at last, it stopped.

They used the lab to herd the sheep
by adding wheels below.

Now everywhere that Mary went,
her lab was sure to go.

They led the sheep to pastures.
Each farmer chose a few.

But Mary had a new idea
she wanted to pursue...

The town was back to normal.
The people were at peace.
Now Mary had a pet and friends...

KNIT-o-Matic

and heaps of snowy fleece.